The Twelve Days of Christmas

Illustrated by Ernie Eldredge

SWEET WATER PRESS

The Twelve Days of Christmas
Copyright © 2005 by Sweetwater Press
Produced by Cliff Road Books

ISBN 1-58173-358-5

Printed in Italy

The Twelve Days of Christmas

On the first day of Christmas,
my true love sent to me ...

a partridge
in a pear tree.

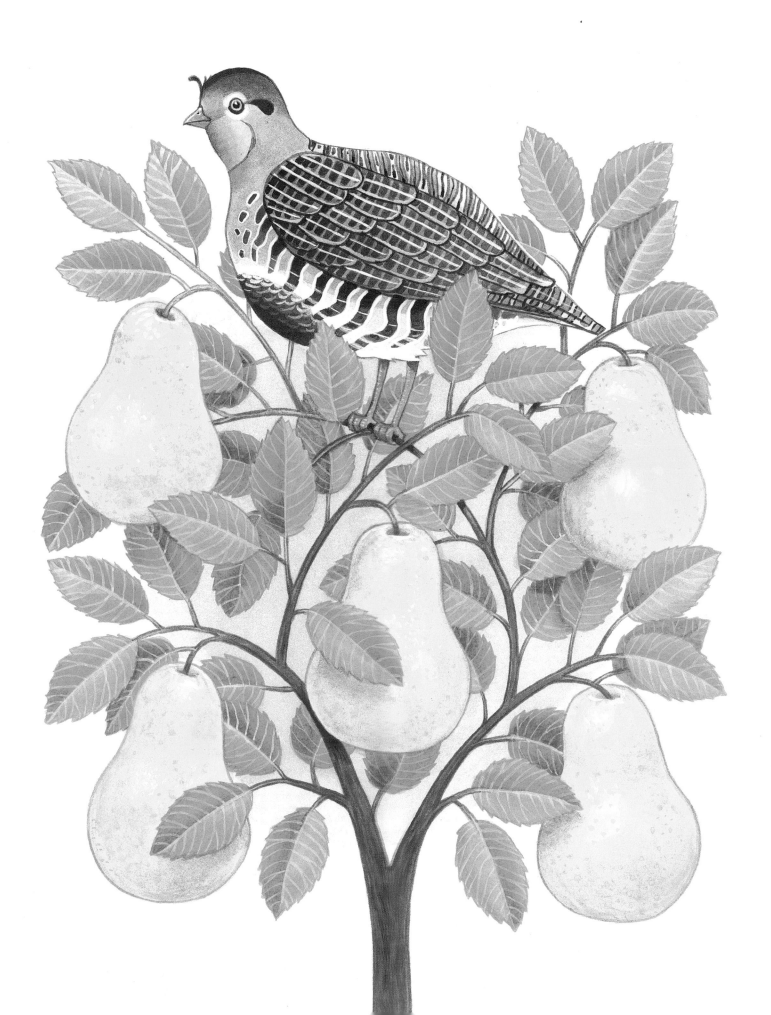

On the second day of Christmas,
my true love sent to me …
two turtledoves
and a partridge in a pear tree.

On the third day of Christmas,
my true love sent to me …
three French hens,
two turtledoves,
and a partridge in a pear tree.

On the fourth day of Christmas,
my true love sent to me ...
four calling birds,
three French hens,
two turtledoves,
and a partridge in a pear tree.

On the fifth day of Christmas,
my true love sent to me …
five gold rings,
four calling birds,
three French hens,
two turtledoves,
and a partridge in a pear tree.

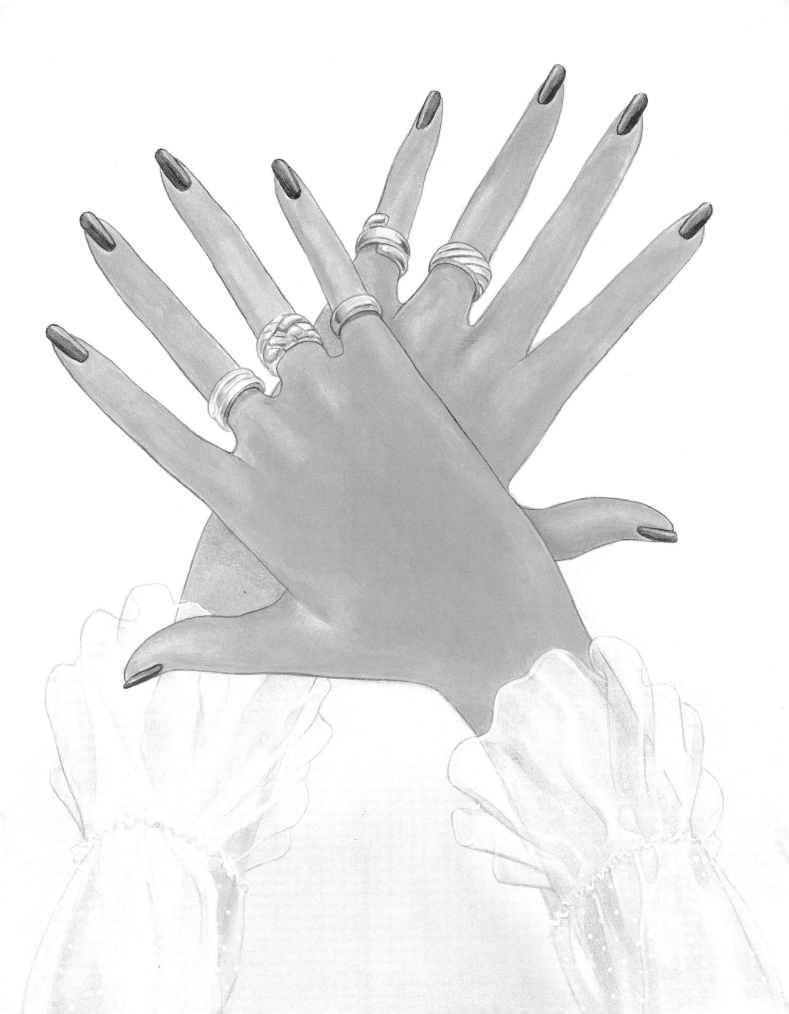

On the sixth day of Christmas,
my true love sent to me …
six geese a-laying,
five gold rings,
four calling birds,
three French hens,
two turtledoves,
and a partridge in a pear tree.

On the seventh day of Christmas,
my true love sent to me ...
seven swans a-swimming,
six geese a-laying,
five gold rings,
four calling birds,
three French hens,
two turtledoves,
and a partridge in a pear tree.

On the eighth day of Christmas,
my true love sent to me …
eight maids a-milking,
seven swans a-swimming,
six geese a-laying,
five gold rings,
four calling birds,
three French hens,
two turtledoves,
and a partridge in a pear tree.

On the ninth day of Christmas,
my true love sent to me …
nine ladies dancing,
eight maids a-milking,
seven swans a-swimming,
six geese a-laying,
five gold rings,
four calling birds,
three French hens,
two turtledoves,
and a partridge in a pear tree.

On the tenth day of Christmas,
my true love sent to me …
ten lords a-leaping,
nine ladies dancing,
eight maids a-milking,
seven swans a-swimming,
six geese a-laying,
five gold rings,
four calling birds,
three French hens,
two turtledoves,
and a partridge in a pear tree.

On the eleventh day of Christmas,
my true love sent to me ...
eleven pipers piping,
ten lords a-leaping,
nine ladies dancing,
eight maids a-milking,
seven swans a-swimming,
six geese a-laying,
five gold rings,
four calling birds,
three French hens,
two turtledoves,
and a partridge in a pear tree.

On the twelfth day of Christmas,
my true love sent to me ...
twelve drummers drumming,
eleven pipers piping,
ten lords a-leaping,
nine ladies dancing,
eight maids a-milking,
seven swans a-swimming,
six geese a-laying,
five gold rings,
four calling birds,
three French hens,
two turtledoves,

and a partridge
in a pear tree.